JEREMY'S SONG

Reading rocks...

LAWRENCE HIGH YEARBOOK SERIES
BOOK III

JEREMY'S SONG

DAVID A. POULSEN

KEY PORTER BOOKS

Library and Archives Canada Cataloguing in Publication

Poulsen, David A., 1946-
    Jeremy's song / David A. Poulsen.

(Lawrence High yearbook series ; 3)
Originally published: Red Deer, Alta. : Coolreading.com, 2001.
ISBN 978-1-55470-098-1

    I. Title. II. Series: Poulsen, David A., 1946- . Lawrence High yearbook series ; 3.

PS8581.O848J47 2008   jC813'.54   C2008-902207-6

The Canada Council | Le Conseil des Arts
for the Arts | du Canada
since 1957 | depuis 1957

ONTARIO ARTS COUNCIL
CONSEIL DES ARTS DE L'ONTARIO

The publisher gratefully acknowledges the support of the Canada Council for the Arts and the Ontario Arts Council for its publishing program. We acknowledge the support of the Government of Ontario through the Ontario Media Development Corporation's Ontario Book Initiative.

We acknowledge the financial support of the Government of Canada through the Book Publishing Industry Development Program (BPIDP) for our publishing activities.

Key Porter Books Limited
Six Adelaide Street East, Tenth Floor
Toronto, Ontario
Canada M5C 1H6

www.keyporter.com

Text design: Marijke Friesen
Electronic formatting: Alison Carr

Printed and bound in Canada

08 09 10 11 12 5 4 3 2 1

In memory of Lloyd Erickson,
who instilled his love of music
in all of his students

1

It wasn't exactly the sound I was expecting to hear.

I mean, there I was on my way to the washroom, and as I was passing room 313, I heard the sound of a violin.

And this violin wasn't cranking out a little Hedley or Nickelback or even vintage Elton John. Nope, this baby was classical . . . as in classical music.

I know classical music when I hear it. My parents like nothing better than to torture me with the stuff every chance they get—which is why I'm glad headphones were invented.

Not that I knew the name of the tune. It's not

like I'm an expert or anything. Although I have to admit—and I wouldn't tell this to anybody at school—I kind of like classical music once in a while.

Anyway, there I was, cruising past 313, which is the third floor social studies room, when I heard the violin. Of course, I thought right away it had to be a CD by some Italian guy with an unpronounceable name. I stood there listening for a while because, to tell the truth, it was pretty good. I mean, I wasn't about to rush out and buy the CD or anything, because if anybody found out about that my reputation as a jock would be shot. But it was pretty decent music.

After a couple of minutes, I headed off to complete my journey to the far end of the hall. The whole time I was standing in the bathroom, I was thinking how weird it was to be hearing classical music at Lawrence High. This place isn't called the "jock joint" by every other school in the city for nothing. At Lawrence, "Sports 'r' Us," if you know what I mean. Football pretty much rules, with baseball and basketball not far behind. Soccer, volleyball, and tennis are big at Lawrence too, and we even have a couple of junior champion golfers kicking around the place.

What *isn't* big at this school is music. I mean, we have a music program and all, but it isn't what Lawrence is about. We have maybe the worst band on the planet, no glee club, no annual musical, and at assemblies we sing the national anthem without accompaniment because there are only a few kids in the place who can play the piano, and even they suck at it. Of course Mrs. Breeze, the music teacher, can play, but she plays every song, including the national anthem, so slow that a lot of us nod off before the thing is over.

Anyway, as I was washing my hands, I decided I owed it to the reputation of Lawrence to find out which teacher was making an entire room full of students listen to classical music during social. And I figured it was worth a few more minutes away from math to check it out.

My plan was to walk into 313 and then pretend I'd gone into the wrong room by accident. I figured I'd get a bit of a chuckle and find out who the classical music freak was. If I was real lucky, Arlene Mitchell might even be in there. Any day that I saw Arlene was a good day.

At Lawrence we have three social teachers: Mr. Goplen, Mr. Dibble, and Mr. Meiklejohn. I take grade ten social from Mr. Dibble, and he seems fairly normal to me so I doubted that he was the Symphony Man. It had to be one of the other two.

Unfortunately, I didn't get a chance to try out my strategy. Just as I got back to 313, the door opened and out came Jeremy Van Pelt. I'd seen Jeremy around the school, but we didn't really hang out or anything. He was a "niner," and, well, enough said. What I did know was that his brother Chris was one of the two or three best hockey players in the city.

Anyway, as Jeremy came out of 313, I got a look inside. There was nobody in there but Mrs. Breeze. And as Jeremy came out of that room, I noticed he was carrying a violin case.

Afterwards, I thought of lots of cool lines I could have used. But right at that moment, all I could come up with was, "That was really good."

Jeremy stopped and looked back at me for a few seconds and sort of smiled. Then he walked off down the hall.

2

I guess that brings us to me. My name is Brad Murray. I'm a tenth grader—a tall and skinny tenth grader. That tall and skinny part is one of those good news/bad news things.

The good news is I play first base for the Lawrence Cowboys baseball team. A lot of baseball coaches like tall first basemen, and I guess it also doesn't hurt that I'm hitting just under .350 and leading the team in RBIs. I love baseball, and like a gazillion guys my age, I'd like to play at a fairly high level. I'm not even talking about The Show—if you're not a big baseball fan, "The Show" is what ball players call the major leagues. I doubt I'll ever get there, but AA or AAA would rock.

I'd at least like to get a scholarship, and things are looking promising in that department. Last year, the coaches from Arizona State and Nebraska came to our school and saw me play. They both said I should have no trouble getting a scholarship when I graduate. A couple of Canadian schools have shown some interest too.

The bad news is that girls don't seem to dig tall and skinny. At least the girls at Lawrence don't. Especially Arlene Mitchell, who is President of the Students' Union, on the Senior Girls Volleyball team, and drop-dead gorgeous. And she goes out with an un-tall, un-skinny guy named Gary Riverton.

I'm not a Gary Riverton fan. The guy seems a little creepy, if you ask me. They say he's a pretty good defenceman for the Eagles, but I've never seen him play. I'm not a big hockey fan either. But I guess Arlene Mitchell is.

The day after I saw (and heard) Jeremy Van Pelt with his violin, I was sitting in the cafeteria with W.T. Zahara—he plays in a rock band, and his nickname's Wild Thing—and Denny Hillman, one of the bigger guys at Lawrence. We were talking about girls, which is what we usually talk about at lunchtime, when we're not talking about sports or cars.

They were giving me totally useless advice about how I could get Arlene to go out with me. I really didn't think pretending to get hit by her mother's car after school, or an exploding baseball bat filled with hundreds of notes that say "I love you, Arlene" were exactly excellent suggestions.

They had just come up with a new idea. This one had something to do with me having myself delivered to her house by a courier truck—which was just as stupid as their other suggestions. I was about to tell them how dumb the idea was when I noticed Jeremy Van Pelt sit down across the table from me and get out his lunch.

He didn't say anything to me, and I was kind of busy with my two hilarious friends, so I didn't say anything either. And to tell the truth, I'd pretty much forgotten about the violin thing, which I suppose says something about my attention span.

After a while, Wild Thing and Denny got up to go. "You better stay here, Brad," said Denny. "There's a chance we might run into some girls, and we don't want you to have a panic attack."

"Hilarious, dude. I'm getting a stomach ache from laughing," I said, but I guess they weren't kidding. They were gone before I could pack up my lunch.

3

I took a bite out of my apple, and that's when I noticed Jeremy looking at me. It got uncomfortable after a while. I was thinking I had mayonnaise on my face or something.

"What?" I said. I didn't sound too friendly, but hey, the guy was only a niner.

Jeremy leaned forward. "Uh...about yesterday. ...I was wondering...did you mean what you said?"

"Huh?" I honestly didn't know what he was talking about. (Remember what I said about attention span?)

"About my music. You said it sounded good."

"Oh." It finally came back to me. "Uh...yeah, sure...it was okay."

"I was wondering if you'd do me a favor."

My immediate thought was, *Whoa I don't even know this kid … what does he want?* But I didn't want to be rude. "I don't know. What do you want?"

"I'd appreciate it if you didn't tell a lot of people that I play the violin, you know? I just … don't want everybody to know."

That blew me away. "Why not? You're really good!"

"Most people don't think it's so great to be able to play the violin."

"Serious? Like who?"

"Uh … just a lot of people."

I nodded. I mean, this was Lawrence High. "Hey, well, no problem. I won't say anything, but I don't think you should be keeping it a secret."

Jeremy started packing up his lunch. "Yeah, well …, thanks."

I almost didn't see her slide in next to me. But when I glanced to my right, who was suddenly sitting there but Arlene Mitchell. My heart did a couple of belly flops and I was working real hard at getting my mouth to say something … anything … but Arlene beat me to it.

"Hi, Jeremy. How ya doin'?"

I couldn't believe it. The girl of my dreams was sitting there talking to a fiddle-playing niner like they were old pals.

"Hey, Arlene, what's up?" Jeremy said.

"When's the big recital?" Arlene asked.

"There's two," Jeremy said. "The first one is a week from Thursday, and the big one at the Jubilee Auditorium is next month."

"Nervous?"

"Yeah, a little," Jeremy smiled. "Especially about the one at the Jubilee. I've never played in front of three thousand people before."

"No worries," Arlene patted his hand. "You'll be great. And I'll be there to cheer you on." She stood up. "See you, Jeremy. See you, Brad."

Whoa ... *see you Brad*? Arlene Mitchell spoke to me! Okay, she didn't pat my hand, and it wasn't exactly a conversation, but she did speak to me. In other words, Arlene Mitchell, the girl I most wanted to spend the rest of my life with, or at least take out on a date, knew I was alive.

It had been a very good day.

4

The Central Composite Bears were an easy team to hate. First of all, they were good ... very good. We'd played them three times already this season, and they'd hammered us each and every time. And we're not that bad. I mean, considering we have only three seniors on our team, we're doing okay. And next year, we should whale on everybody ... including Central.

The Bears are also very arrogant. They're the only team in our league that does any trash-talking. They start playing with our heads before the game even begins, and they keep it up until the last out is made.

And their little mind games work pretty well

too. Especially with me. I don't know why, but I play like a jerk every time our two teams meet. This game was no exception. We were into the seventh inning, and I was 0 for 2 with a strikeout and a pop fly. And I'd booted a grounder that a grade-school kid could have handled.

We were down 5-1, even though our pitcher, Ricky Lyons, had been throwing bullets. He hadn't been getting much help so far, but suddenly things were looking up. We had guys on second and third with nobody out. A base hit now and we'd be right back in it.

There was only one problem. I was up. Dwight Kincaid was pitching for the Bears, and I was maybe zero for a million against him. Going all the way back to Little League, Kincaid had had my number.

I figured Coach Bunning was probably thinking about yanking me for a pinch hitter. But he didn't. I appreciated that, and really wanted to get a hit to pay him back.

As I stepped up to the plate, Kincaid was grinning. In fact, several of the Bears were grinning. Their catcher's name was—Tom Cruz, no kidding, that was his name, different spelling but *that* name. Cruz was a giant, even when he was squatting behind the plate. He was grinning and talking.

"Well, look who we have here. Ol' Babe Ruth himself. Or is it Lou Gehrig? Oh no, it couldn't be any of those fellas ... they actually hit the ball. Oh, now I recognize you. It's ol' Rally Killer, that's who. Like the kid in the comic strip ... who was it? Oh yeah, Charlie Brown. Yeah, that's right. He never hit the ball either. Well, step up there, Killer, and get it over with. Hey, anybody ever tell you it's okay to have actual meat on your body? Who knows, if you had some meat, maybe you'd even get some muscles happening."

There was a lot more, but you get the general idea. I hate to admit it, but I found myself actually paying attention to what he was saying. Which was not a good idea when you were about to face Dwight Kincaid. There aren't many guys in high school that can throw the 90-mile-an-hour heater. But Kincaid could. And did. On top of that, he had a wicked curve and a decent slider. If there was a guy I'd ever seen who had "The Show" written all over him, it was Kincaid.

I stepped in and was 0 and 2 before I even got the bat off my shoulder. I stepped out to think about things. Kincaid had thrown two fastballs, both right down the middle. One thing I knew for sure—even though we were in the seventh inning, Kincaid wasn't slowing down any.

I happened to glance over at the crowd, which is something I almost never do. And there in about the second row, was Arlene. She was sitting with her boyfriend, Gary, and on the other side of her was Jeremy Van Pelt. What was the deal with her and Jeremy? I mean, I knew they weren't boyfriend/girlfriend, or they wouldn't have been sitting there with Gary Riverton. I guessed they must just be friends. For a second, I wished my mom and dad had started me on the violin instead of baseball when I was little.

Instead, I was about to strike out with runners on base, in front of the girl I was nuts about. Definitely not impressive. Maybe Cruz was right about the Charlie Brown thing. I was starting to feel like a loser.

5

I got my mind back on the game. I'd already seen two fastballs, and the logical thing was for Kincaid to get me to chase a breaking ball. But these were the Bears, and this was Kincaid. We're talking Major League ego here. I figured he'd love nothing better than to blow three fastballs by me just to make me look bad.

I decided to look for the fastball. If he threw me the curve, I'd look like an idiot. But what the heck? I'd pretty well looked that way for the entire game so far, so I didn't think I had all that much to lose. I stepped in, tapped the ground with the end of my bat, and looked out at the mound. Cruz was still yapping behind the plate, but I had him pretty well tuned-out.

Kincaid shook off the first sign. I hoped like crazy it was the curve ball. He nodded, checked the runners and went into his windup. He let it go.

There's a sound a bat makes when you hit the ball right on the sweet spot—just about where the words "Louisville Slugger" go. That was the sound I heard as I made contact with a Kincaid fastball—right down the middle.

I hit it good and I knew it. The ball headed for the gap in right center. It went to the wall, and I was into second with a stand-up double and two runs batted in. I looked over at the bleachers. Arlene and Jeremy were both standing up cheering big time. Riverton was way too cool to cheer, so he just sat there looking bored.

I stood on second base and clapped my hands. "Guess the curve would've been a better idea," I yelled at Kincaid, who was making a point of not looking at me. Normally, I don't get into the yapping-at-the-other-team thing, but this time I had a couple of things to say. "Chalk one up for ol' Rally Killer," I called to Cruz, who had his mask off and was looking pretty ticked at Kincaid.

I guess my double must have thrown Kincaid off his game, because he walked our next hitter, and then Jeff Sandvick took him deep with a three-run homer. Our bullpen held them off the rest of the way, and we knocked off the Bears for the first time in two seasons. I didn't care if we beat them again for the rest of the season—I really just wanted that one.

After the game we celebrated like crazy and some of our fans even came down onto the field to join in. Arlene stopped in front of me and smiled that million-dollar smile of hers. "Great game, Brad. Clutch hit."

That clinched it. Not only did this woman look sensational, she used words like "clutch" and knew what they meant. She was perfect.

I tried to say something memorable, but all I could come up with was "Uh ... thanks." I don't think I dazzled her with my conversational skills.

Jeremy was there too, and shook my hand. "Awright! You guys put it to Central. That's awesome."

I found myself liking this kid more all the time. For a niner, he was okay.

When the on-field celebration was over, all the guys on the team headed for Shakey's Pizza and Ginger Beef Garage. It was the Lawrence High social spot. Coach Bunning was buying the shakes. Life was starting to look better all the time. Maybe I wasn't Charlie Brown after all.

6

The next day at school, about halfway through English, I made a decision. I was going to ask Arlene Mitchell out.

Sure, there was the little matter of the boyfriend, but I decided not to let that stop me. For one thing, the guy was a jerk. For another, maybe once Arlene knew I was interested, she'd decide to ditch the grumpy hockey jock for the tall, skinny baseball player.

At least that was my thinking going into English class. Right up until Mr. White asked me a question about the importance of ambition as a theme in *Macbeth*. My answer wasn't going to win me a Nobel Prize for literature, but I got by.

I was seriously glad I'd read the play.

It's funny how an idea that seems so good in English class can become so utterly stupid by the time lunch rolls around. It's one thing to decide to ask a girl out ... it's a whole different deal to actually *do* it.

I was having lunch with Wild Thing and Denny again, and they were still offering helpful suggestions as to how I could get Arlene to notice me. I had already rejected skydiving into her backyard during a family barbecue, then telling her I was working undercover for the CIA and that Gary was a suspected terrorist.

That's when I saw Arlene in the food line. Normally, I wouldn't have done anything except stare at her and wish I had the courage to ask her out. But when W.T. and Denny started making very loud chicken noises, I figured I had no choice. I knew they'd keep it up until she heard them, and decided all three of us were idiots.

I butted into the line so I could get close to Arlene. Of course, there was the usual "Back of the line, Butthead" type comments, but everybody settled down when I said I just needed a plastic fork. I got to Arlene just as she arrived at the cashier. The cashier's name was Lois. She'd been working in the school cafeteria for about twenty years, and could be pretty grumpy sometimes. Mostly she liked sarcasm. I guess if you've been around high school students for that long, you might just get a little sarcastic.

I took a deep breath. "Uh ... hi Arlene."

She looked back at me. "Oh, hi Brad."

"Hello, Brad," Lois said. "That'll be $2.40."

"For a plastic fork?" I guess I was a little nervous.

"For her salad and juice, Professor," Lois said.

"Yeah, right." I turned to Arlene. "Uh ... I was wondering if maybe you'd like to go out sometime.... You know ..., with me," I said.

"I don't think so ... you're cute, but a little young," Lois said.

"No ... I mean ... I was talking to Arlene."

"No kidding," Lois said.

They were both laughing, and I had a feeling this wasn't going well. Arlene handed Lois a five dollar bill.

"Uh ... maybe next Friday?" I tried to get the

conversation back on track.

"Two-sixty change," Lois said, as she handed Arlene the money.

"Thanks," Arlene said.

"You're welcome," I said and Lois and Arlene laughed again.

"Oh … you were thanking her … I mean…." I tried laughing too, but it came out like a hysterical cackle. "So, uh … well … what about next Friday?"

"I'd really like to, but I'm seeing someone right now … and anyway, I'm going to Jeremy's violin recital that night."

"Oh … uh … yeah, well, that's okay then … thanks anyway," I started to walk away.

"Unless you'd like to go with me. I mean, it wouldn't be like you were taking me out exactly, so I guess it would be okay."

"Yeah, great … uh … Jeremy's recital sounds fine. I'll see you after school and we can talk about it."

I started to walk away again.

"Hey, Professor, don't forget your plastic fork."

I looked back at Lois, and this time all three of us laughed. Hey, I was about to spend an evening with Arlene Mitchell—even if I wasn't actually taking her out, and even if it was a violin recital. This was good. This was real good.

As I headed back to my table, even the chicken noises—which were louder than ever—didn't bother me.

7

I wasn't sure how I was supposed to dress. I don't like suits, and anyway I think I look like a stuffed stork in one. So I was totally relieved when mom and dad said I would be okay in dress pants and a sweater. But just to be on the safe side, I decided to wear a shirt and tie under the sweater.

I didn't want to look out of place at the concert, but most of all I didn't want to look like a total geek to Arlene. I'd never been in the Central high school gym before, which is where the concert was. The gym was decorated, and there were giant curtains hanging all around the place. Up until that moment, my idea of a gym had been a place where people went to gym class, and where there were basketball games on Friday nights.

Arlene had caught a ride to Central with her mom, and I had taken the bus. It wasn't the most romantic way to start an evening, but I didn't care. I was just happy that I was going to be with her once I got there.

I saw Arlene talking to some people just inside the front doors. She looked spectacular in a sort of cream coloured dress that made her eyes seem even bluer than usual. When she saw me, she turned away from the people she was standing with and smiled at me. We said "hi" and "how you doing." Then I said, "Wow, this place hardly even looks like a gymnasium."

"Gyms are notorious for bad acoustics," she said. "They're hoping the curtains will help."

"Yeah … sure … I hope so too, I guess." I hadn't thought much about acoustics before that. I figured Jeremy would just get out there and play his violin, and that was that. I had a few things to learn.

One of the things I had to learn was how to talk to Arlene. I kept getting tongue-tied, especially if I made the mistake of looking at her eyes. The woman had great eyes. And every time I looked at them, the main word in my vocabulary became "uh." As in "So ... uh ... Arlene ... uh ... how are you ... uh ... doing?" Talk about *stupid*.

Then there was the music part of the evening. Like I said before, I really don't mind classical music. But I'm also not going to rush out and download the *Every Song Mozart Ever Wrote* collection. So, I guess you could say I was pretty bummed when I found out Jeremy wasn't even going to play until the second half of the recital. I tried telling myself that must mean he's really good, and the other people are like the warm-up act at a Sum 41 concert.

But to tell the truth, I had sort of been hoping that Jeremy would do his thing and then Arlene and I could slide over to Shakey's and get to know each other a little better. But, nope, first there was a girl with glasses thicker than Coke bottles. She played what sounded like funeral songs on the piano. Next came a tall, skinny guy (even taller and skinnier than me) who sang opera about the same way I sing it when I'm fooling around in the shower. Then there was another girl. I thought this one was cute (until I found out she went to Central) and she played the flute really well.

Intermission arrived just in time. When I'm nervous, I drink a lot of water. And before my date with Arlene, I was really nervous, so I drank a lot of water. If the cute flute player had played one more song, the situation might have turned ugly. I nearly trampled some people as I raced for the bathroom, and when I got back out into the hallway outside the gymnasium, there was no sign of Arlene. So much for using that opportunity to turn on the Murray charm.

Just as intermission was ending, I spotted Arlene talking on the pay phone. I was willing to bet my dad's pickup she was talking to "the boyfriend." She saw me and smiled and waved. She hung up a few seconds later, and came over. It seemed to me like she was in a really good mood all of a sudden. I was wishing I could think of some brilliant remark that would totally blow Gary out of the water but, of course, I couldn't.

"Ready?" she smiled at me, all perky.

"Sure, why not?" I said, and we headed back into the gymnasium.

8

We sat down, and that's when something really weird happened. We sat there for a minute, and then Jeremy came out on stage. People gave him a little of the ol' polite applause, but nobody announced who he was, and he didn't say anything either. He just started to play. He started slow, and real soft. After a while, the music got louder—well, not really louder—just more intense, or something. But the weird part was, it was one of the neatest things I'd ever heard in my life.

Jeremy must have played for an hour. For a couple of the pieces, the girl with the Coke-bottle glasses came out and played the piano, while Jeremy played his violin. The last piece he played

was even better than all the rest of the stuff he'd
played up until then. I leaned over and whispered
to Arlene, "What's the name of this?"

"Mendelssohn's 'Sixth Violin Concerto,'" she
whispered back.

Remember what I said about the sound a bat
makes when it strikes a baseball just right? Well,
this sound was like that. It was ... a perfect sound.
It was so good, I forgot about how much water I'd
had to drink before the recital, and I even forgot
about Arlene being beside me (well, maybe for
part of the time).

When Jeremy finished playing, and we were
all done standing and clapping like crazy, Arlene
and I sat in our chairs and didn't say anything. We
just sat there.

Finally, Arlene turned to me and said, "Thank
you."

"For what?"

"For coming here tonight ... and for ... liking
it." I guess she'd been able to tell.

"It was great ... I mean, it really was great."

A couple of minutes later, Jeremy came out
into the gymnasium and some of us gathered

around him to tell him how much we had enjoyed it. When he saw me he grinned, "Hey, First Baseman, I didn't expect to see you here."

"You were awesome, man," I told him.

"Thanks." Jeremy turned to Arlene. "I told you he was a cool guy."

I think Arlene was kind of embarrassed when he said that, but she smiled at both of us. I was watching Jeremy, and I noticed he kept looking around. It was like he was looking for someone. Arlene introduced me to his mom, and a couple of minutes later we figured it was time to go.

"See you at school tomorrow," I told him.

"Yeah, I'll see you guys," he said, but I could tell he was still looking around at the people who hadn't left yet.

9

We got outside, I asked Arlene if she'd noticed it too. "Of course," she answered. "He was looking for his dad."

"He wasn't here?"

"No way. Not if his other son had a hockey game."

Like I said, Chris Van Pelt was good, and was already attracting a lot of attention from pro hockey scouts.

"It must be neat having one kid who's a great hockey player, and one who can play the violin like that," I said.

"Nick Van Pelt has only one son," Arlene said quietly.

"What do you mean?"

"The reason Jeremy couldn't see his dad, is because he wasn't there. He's never there." She sounded sort of half sad and half mad as she said it.

"I still don't get it," I said.

"Mr. Van Pelt never misses any of Chris's games." Arlene started down the street, and I fell in alongside her. "He even goes to most of his practices. But he's never been to even one of Jeremy's music performances. Not a recital, not a concert, nothing."

We hadn't talked about how we were getting home. I was hoping we might walk, and it looked like Arlene had the same idea. Riding the bus with Arlene wasn't really my idea of a romantic way to end the evening, even though it was a crisp night that reminded me winter wasn't far off.

"Not even one?" I shook my head. "I can't believe that. You're kidding, right?"

Arlene wasn't kidding. She didn't say anything for quite a while, and when she spoke again, I was pretty surprised at how angry she was. "What a scumbag!" She slammed the little purse she was carrying against her leg.

"Are you ... uh ... warm enough?" I asked her.

She smiled at me. "Yeah, I'm fine. Sorry, I didn't mean to get mad, it's just that ..."

"It's okay," I smiled back at her. "Have you and Jeremy ... uh ... been friends for a long time?" I hoped she didn't think I was getting too snoopy or anything.

"Since grade school. I used to be his reading buddy when I was in fourth grade and he was in first." Arlene answered. "We even played in the school band together. Jeremy played the tambourine and I played the triangle. We were awesome," she laughed. Arlene had a great laugh, kind of throaty, and when you put the laugh together with the great eyes, she was pretty spectacular.

"We've been friends all through school," Arlene added, "so I know how much it would mean to him for his dad to come to one of his music things ... just one. He doesn't say anything, or if he does, he makes excuses for his dad. You know, 'I'm sure Dad would have been here, but the boss probably kept him late. He'll be there next time ... he told me.' I've heard him say stuff like that for years. I guess it's hard to admit your dad just doesn't care."

I'd never really thought about that. My parents have come to most of my stuff: ball games, Christmas concerts, I was even in a play once in eighth grade. I was pretty bad, but my parents were both there and, of course, they said I was the next Matt Damon.

"Yeah, that would be really tough," I nodded. We didn't talk for quite a while, and when we did, we both started talking at once. Have you ever noticed how that happens? Nobody says anything for maybe three minutes, and then at the exact same second, both people start talking. Weird.

Then, of course, we both said, "You go ahead ... no, you go ahead" until we sounded like two of the Three Stooges. Arlene laughed again, which made the whole thing worth it.

I decided I'd better say something before we started the routine all over. "Uh ... I was wondering ... you know ... if you and Gary are ... you know ... serious."

Arlene looked at me and smiled. Not a big

smile, but enough of one that I figured she didn't mind me asking. "I don't know," she said. "I'm not sure I'd say we're serious, exactly, but we've been going out for almost a year now."

"So, I guess you like him then."

"Well, yeah, but lately he's been getting very possessive. Like telling me I spend too much time with my girlfriends, or with Jeremy ... stuff like that. I don't like that a whole lot."

I grinned at her. "So I guess he'll be really excited about you and me being at the concert together."

"I told him you were going to be there," Arlene said, which almost blew me away. "I told him you're my friend, and that I'd be seeing you at the concert, that's all."

"How'd he take that?" I was hoping she'd say he threatened to break up with her.

"He didn't say much," she shrugged her shoulders.

After that we talked baseball some—Arlene knew a lot about the game—and about school; the stuff you'd expect people to talk about when they're just getting to know each other. By the time we got to her house, I have to admit I was feeling pretty good about the way the evening had gone.

I didn't try to kiss her. I figured that could blow the whole thing. I was very cool—said goodnight and told her I had a great time. She said about the same thing, and it was over. But I walked off feeling like I'd just won one of those Super Lottos. I was feeling *great*.

10

We were playing the Western Composite Vipers. They were a good team—not like Central, but pretty good just the same. It was a big game for both schools because of a rivalry that dated back about thirty years.

Each team had a graduate go to the big leagues back then. They'd played against each other in high school, and wound up facing each other again in the 1977 World Series. Matt Tucker came out of our school and was a utility infielder for the Yankees that year. That was the year Reggie Jackson hit three homers in the seventh game for the Yanks. Rory Huddleston was a pitcher for Western, and was a reliever for the L.A. Dodgers in the same Series.

Ever since that World Series, the thing between the two schools has been pretty intense. The year after, our team started wearing pinstripes like the Yankees. A year later, Western changed their uniforms to look like the Dodgers. That sort of tells you the kind of thinking that's happening here. Personally, I think it's all kind of juvenile. But I have to admit I get into it once the game starts.

We play the Vipers three times each season, and if we split the first two games, like we did this year, that third game—the one we were about to play—can get pretty crazy. Of course, before the game I checked the stands to see if I could see Arlene anywhere. I couldn't, but that didn't mean she wasn't there. The stands were always packed for the Western games, and that meant there were about two thousand faces out there.

We started strong. Our pitcher, John Neis, had great stuff, and struck out eight guys in the first five innings. But their guy, a tall kid who was all arms and legs, was pretty good too. We had base runners in four of the first five innings, but couldn't get anything across. I left two runners stranded in the third, when I struck out on a slow curve that made me look bad.

In the top of the sixth, Western got a run after John walked the leadoff man. The next hitter sacrificed him to second, and then I booted a slow-roller that made the one Bill Buckner muffed in the World Series look like a screaming line drive. I made up for it a couple of minutes later. The Vipers loaded the bases, and their cleanup man drilled one down the first base line that would have gone for extra bases. I dived and snagged it, then rolled to the bag and got there just in time to double the runner off. We got out of the inning only down one, and feeling pretty good about ourselves.

There was one weird thing about that inning. The guy who hit the line drive kept coming down the first base line, even though he saw me catch the ball before he even got out of the batter's box. When I got my hand on first for the double play, I happened to look up. It's a good thing I did, because he nearly got me with his spikes. If I hadn't got my head out of the way at the last second, this pretty face that drives women insane would have been a lot less pretty.

I jumped up to say something to the guy, but the first base umpire headed me off. The guy went back to his dugout without even looking at me. I figured maybe he was just a little intense, and I'd let it go—once.

In our half of the sixth, we finally got to their pitcher. We chalked up five runs, including two when I hit my tenth homer of the season. It was kind of a cheapy; it barely made it over the left field fence, but I'll take it.

Our fans were having a really good time, and when I looked over at the stands again, I saw Arlene. She gave me a big smile and waved. Jeremy was on the other side of her, high-fiving everybody around him. The best part was, I didn't see Gary.

I didn't have time to think about what that meant, if anything, because our second baseman, French, popped out, and we had to take the field. Actually, his name is Marcel Boileau, but everybody calls him French because he comes from Quebec. Anyway, after French popped out, I grabbed my glove and started running out to first base. That's when the second weird thing happened.

As the Vipers ran off the field, the third baseman—the guy who'd tried to slice and dice my
face—ran over to the dugout and started talking
to someone who was leaning over the fence. That
would have been no big deal, except that the guy
he was talking to was Gary Riverton. That's
when I noticed the name on the back of the third
baseman's jersey. It was Riverton, too.

11

I remembered somebody telling me that there were two Riverton brothers. It was a split-parents deal, with Gary living with his dad and going to Lawrence, and the brother—I remembered his first name was Tyler—living across town with his mom and going to Western. Now, here they were, having a heart to heart at the ol' ball game. I was starting to wonder if the "step-on-the-first-baseman" incident was a coincidence. Especially after I saw the two brothers looking at me, with Gary pointing and nodding.

John Neis got roughed up a little that inning. He gave up a walk and two doubles, and the Vipers had a run in and men on second and third, with only one out. Coach Bunning decided to bring in a reliever. He went to Ricky Lyons, who's probably our best pitcher. I think the coach wanted to win this game as bad as we did.

The first guy Ricky would face was—guess who?—Tyler Riverton. While Ricky was throwing his warm-up tosses, I looked over behind the Vipers' dugout to see if Gary Riverton was still there. He wasn't. I wondered if he'd gone up to sit with Arlene, but I didn't have time to check that out.

Ricky, who normally has great control, walked Riverton on four pitches. With the bases loaded, Coach Bunning didn't want me holding the runner on, but I walked over close to the bag anyway.

"Try to spike me again and I'll re-arrange both of your brain cells." I said it softly, just loud enough so Tyler could make out the words. Riverton started toward me right away, but their first base coach got between us before anything could happen. Coach Bunning must have seen what was happening, because he called time out and ran onto the field.

I figured I was in deep then; Coach Bunning isn't somebody to fool around with. He's a pretty serious guy, and when it comes to baseball, he gets extra serious. To make matters worse, he had warned us at the start of the season that he wouldn't tolerate any charging the mound or clearing the dugout.

He stood close to me so nobody could hear what he was saying. "What's going on, Brad?"

"You saw what he did before," I answered. "I was just telling him what would happen if he tried to run me again."

Coach Bunning didn't look real happy, but he didn't look totally mad either. "Just play baseball and leave the rest of it alone. If he tries anything, the umpires will look after it, or I will."

As Coach turned and ran off the field, I looked over at Riverton. He was grinning at me. I walked back to my spot behind first base.

Ricky went to three and two on the next hitter. His next pitch was a dandy curve ball that the guy hit high in the air to center field. It was an easy play for Jeff Sandvick, and I went over to the bag in case Riverton went too far off and we got a shot at doubling him off.

And that's exactly what happened. Riverton went about half way to second, which was pretty stupid, since there was no way Sandvick was going to drop that fly ball. Jeff is pretty sharp and saw that we had a shot at Riverton. Plus, he's got a real good arm. He fired a strike to me, and I could see it would be close.

I was too busy watching the throw coming in to keep a close eye on Riverton. I figured he'd either dive or slide, and I stretched to get the throw. That's when the pain hit me.

All of a sudden, it felt like my ankle was on fire. I caught the ball and heard the umpire yell "out," and the next thing I knew, I was rolling around on the ground holding my ankle. When I finally pulled my hands away and looked down, I saw that my foot and lower leg were covered with blood. This time, Riverton had gotten me with his spikes.

I was so mad that I actually got up on my one good foot and tried to get at the guy. "You stupid son-of-a——!"

I wouldn't have been able to get to him

hopping around on one foot, except that he came closer to try to give me another shot. I beat him to it, and I have to admit I enjoyed the sound that came from his nose as my fist made contact. I don't know if I broke it or not, but I definitely did it some harm. Riverton went down and did some rolling around of his own.

Of course, by then there were umpires and coaches and other players all milling around, and the fight was over. Not that I would have been able to fight any more anyway, because my ankle gave out and I went down.

12

They had to take me to the hospital, and I got twenty-four stitches in my lower leg where Riverton's spikes had done their damage. Both of us were suspended for the next two games. That didn't mean much to me, because I wouldn't have been able to play anyway.

We ended up winning that game 8-4, but when the guys came by the hospital to tell me that, I didn't much care. They were going on about how great they thought it was that I'd nailed Riverton. I didn't think it was all that great. Maybe it makes me a nerd or a wimp or something, but I'm not a believer in violence in sports—I even did a paper on it in English. And now here I was, no better than all the dorks I'd written about. Even though I was sure Riverton was out to get me, I was wishing I hadn't lost it and thrown that punch.

But the worst part of the whole day came before they even took me off the field. That's when I looked into the stands and saw Arlene. She didn't even look at me, and the expression on her face suggested she was less than thrilled. I figured any chance I had with her went out the window with my James Bond impersonation.

I was able to go to school the next day, although I had to use crutches. They told me I'd have to use them for a few days. A lot of the kids at school were treating me like I was a hero, though mostly I just wished they'd leave me alone. I was hoping to get a chance to talk to Arlene, but I didn't. She wasn't in the lunch area at noon. That meant I got to spend some more quality time with Denny and Wild Thing. They had a new idea. They thought I should make a trophy of my blood-soaked shoe and the ripped lower pant leg of my baseball uniform and present it to Arlene as a "love gesture."

Usually I was able to laugh at their insane

suggestions, but not this time. I was really worried that Arlene and I were history. To top it off, I
saw Gary as I was coming out of the computer lab.

"Hey, Murray, what's your problem anyway?
Can't take a little physical contact out there? Sure
glad you don't play hockey. We'd have to change
the rules to make it non-contact so little Brad
wouldn't get hurt."

There were a lot of things I wanted to say, but
I figured I'd be better off keeping my mouth shut.
As I hopped off on my crutches, I could hear him
laughing. It was all I could do to keep from going
back and giving him a crutch-whack on the side
of the head. But I was sure that any chance I had
with Arlene would be officially dead if I did
something stupid again.

After school, I saw Jeremy standing on the
front steps of the school. He came over and
grinned at me. "How you doin', Killer?"

"Okay, I guess," I didn't return the grin.

He seemed to figure out I wasn't in the mood
for humor. "How's the ankle?"

"The ankle's fine," I said. "It's my brain that
needs work."

"What do you mean?"

"Well, I doubt if Arlene was too impressed with my performance."

"I don't know," he shook his head. "She hasn't really said much."

"You know something, Jeremy? I have a feeling big brother Gary was behind what happened." We started walking—hopping—down the stairs. "How else would his brother have known me?" I told him about seeing the two Riverton brothers huddled up and talking during the game.

Jeremy nodded. "It's possible, all right. You want me to mention that to Arlene for you?"

"No way," I shook my head. "It wouldn't do any good anyway. I still acted like a jerk out there."

"Hey, you coming to my concert Wednesday night?" Jeremy asked. "This is the big one."

"I don't know …" I said.

"That's okay," he said real fast. "I know you're probably busy. It's no big deal." He walked off before I could say anything else. My day, which had pretty much sucked up till then, suddenly seemed even worse.

13

I wish I could say I'd decided to go to Jeremy's concert for unselfish reasons. But the truth is, I thought if I saw Arlene there, I might get a chance to talk to her. And if she saw me at a concert on my own, maybe she'd decide I was an okay guy after all.

Of course, there was always the possibility that she'd realize I was doing the whole thing for selfish reasons, and hate me even more. I tried to put that thought out of my head. My love life, if you could even call it that, was becoming very confusing. And I was starting to feel more like Charlie Brown all the time.

Anyway, I decided to go hear Jeremy play. I went with the sweater-over-the-shirt-and-tie look again. Before I left the house, I checked myself out in the mirror. I thought I looked not too bad. No chance of being mistaken for Brad Pitt—but decent, given what I had to work with.

I got to the Jubilee Auditorium about twenty minutes before the start of the concert, hoping that maybe Arlene would be hanging around the lobby. She wasn't. And it might have been hard to find her, anyway. This place was nothing like the high school gymnasium we'd been in for Jeremy's first concert.

I got myself a bottled water, and sat on a big sofa. For a while, I just checked out the crowd. I was glad I'd decided to dress up a bit, because I wasn't seeing a lot of jeans and sweatshirts.

I was sitting on the sofa enjoying my water when a very big lady sat beside me. I mean, she was big all over. Her husband sat down on the other side of her, and they started talking about some people they knew. Most of what they were saying was pretty nasty. I was staring off into space, wondering if it would be rude if I got up and moved away. I guess that's why I didn't see Arlene. She was right beside me before I noticed her.

"Hi, Brad," she said.

I stood up. "Uh ... hi Arlene." *Already with the "uh,"* I thought to myself.

"I was wondering ... could I speak to you?" Arlene looked serious—no, more than serious. She looked worried.

"Sure," I said, and we moved away from the sofa and over to the huge windows that looked out over the city. For a couple of minutes, we stared out at the headlights of the cars going by the street next to the auditorium.

"What happened at the ball game?" she said finally.

"You were there," I said. "You saw what happened."

"I saw you get spiked, and I saw you punch Matt. But Jeremy told me there was more to it." She turned and looked at me. "Was there?"

"What do you mean?"

"Did you get into a fight with Matt because he's Gary's brother?"

I shook my head. "I didn't even know they were brothers until halfway through the game. Besides, why would I get into a fight with somebody's brother? If I didn't like Gary, it would make more sense to get into a fight with him."

"So, do you like Gary?"

"Well, actually ... no."

And suddenly we both looked at each other and laughed. When we stopped, Arlene looked at me again, serious this time.

"Do you think Matt tried to hurt you because Gary put him up to it?"

I shrugged. "I honestly don't know."

"I guess we should go in."

"Yeah ... maybe I'll see you at intermission."

"I can't ... I told Jeremy I'd come back and see him before he went on," Arlene said. "But if you want, maybe you could come for coffee after. I mean, it'll be with my parents, so—"

"Coffee would be great," I said way too loud, and quite a few people turned and looked at us.

I went into the seating area, but to tell the truth, I wasn't thinking a whole lot about classical music. This time, there was only one person who played before Jeremy—a girl named Jennifer Puddicombe, who played the cello. I thought she was awesome. After about three

minutes, I was wondering if she might make
Jeremy look bad.

She played for maybe forty-five minutes.
Then a guy with a deep voice came on the public
address system to say there would be a fifteen-
minute intermission before Mr. Jeremy Van Pelt
performed. That's what he said ..., "Mr. Jeremy
Van Pelt." I thought that was pretty cool. I tried
to think if I'd ever heard baseball players referred
to as "Mister." I didn't think so. "Mr. Babe Ruth"
or "Mr. Dizzy Dean" didn't make it, somehow.

I stood around in the lobby part of the auditorium drinking a Sprite and waiting for the
deep-voiced guy to tell us to get back to our seats.
I wondered if Jeremy was nervous. I knew I
would be. No, cancel that. I'd be terrified. About
the time I figured intermission should be ending,
Arlene came running up and grabbed my arm.
"Come on!" she said in a voice that told me something was big-time wrong.

I didn't get it. I looked around, half expecting
to see smoke or something.

"Come on," she said again. "You've got to
come backstage. He says he's not going to play."

"What?"

"He says he's not going to play, and he means it."

"What ... what do you want me to do?" We were running down the aisle that would take us to the backstage area. Well, Arlene was running— I was sort of hobbling as fast as my injured leg would allow.

"Talk to him. He likes you ... maybe he'll listen to you."

I grabbed Arlene's arm, and got her stopped. "Wait a second," I said. "He likes you, and obviously he didn't listen to you, so what makes you think ... why won't he go on? Is he scared?"

"He's not here," she said.

"Huh?"

"His dad. He's not here. He promised he'd come, and Jeremy has been peeking through the curtain the whole first half. All that's out there is an empty seat."

She started pulling me down the aisle again. Just then, Mr. Deep-Voice said, "Our program will resume in three minutes."

Terrific, I thought to myself. I had no idea

what I was going to say that would get Jeremy Van Pelt on stage in three minutes. We got to a door marked Dressing Room 4. Arlene pointed at it and nodded.

"Whoa, hold on. You're coming with me."

She shook her head. "I've been in there already. He needs to hear from somebody else right now." She turned and started down the hall, leaving me looking at the closed dressing room door.

14

I stood there for quite a while, trying to think of what I was going to say when I got in there. Just as I tapped on the door, I heard, "This evening's program will resume in two minutes."

There was no sound from the other side of the door. I tapped again, and pushed it open. I saw Jeremy sitting on a chair in the corner. He looked up, and there were tears running down his face—a lot of tears.

I went over and pulled a chair up so I was sitting facing him. "How's it going, man?" I said.

He looked up at me. A lot of guys would have told me to take a hike, but not Jeremy, even as bad as he was feeling. He didn't say anything, but I've never in my whole life seen anyone look as sad as he looked right then.

"Uh … Jeremy … listen. I … uh … know you thought your dad would be here and he isn't … yet—"

"He isn't coming," he interrupted me.

"Well, maybe he's just running late.... I know my parents are always behind schedule—"

"He's not coming," Jeremy said again. "My brother had a game tonight. An *exhibition* game. He promised he'd come after the first period. But he won't. He won't be here."

"Okay, well, let's say he doesn't show up. There are a lot of people out there who *do* care … who really want to hear you play. You don't want to disappoint them."

"You're wrong, Brad. I don't care if they're disappointed. I really don't care. I'm tired of always being the one …"

He stopped then and looked off over my head.

"Yeah, well, I think I can understand that—"

"No, you can't. You can't understand it at all." He lowered his eyes, and was looking at me now.

"You're an athlete. Your parents … your dad … is proud of you. My dad thinks I'm weird. He thinks anybody who cares about music and isn't good at sports is some kind of wimp. You know what's really crazy? I was good at sports! I could run faster than my brother, and I can still crush him in tennis or one-on-one basketball. I was never as good as he was in hockey, but I wasn't bad. It's just not what I wanted. This …" he looked at his violin, sitting on a table, "this is what I wanted."

And then, suddenly, Jeremy Van Pelt cried. I mean, he'd already been crying but now he broke down … totally. He cried as hard as I've ever seen anybody cry. For a long time we sat there. I had one hand on his shoulder, and I could feel it shaking with every sob. I don't think I ever knew before what people meant when they said someone had a broken heart. But sitting there with Jeremy, I started to understand.

There was a knock at the door. Someone called, "It's time Mr. Van Pelt."

"He'll be a minute," I called back.

"But—"

"I said, he'll be a minute," I was louder that

time, and I heard footsteps going away from the door.

"You're right, Jeremy," I said slowly. "I don't understand. But I know one thing. If you don't play tonight, then he wins. He'll be able to say 'playing the violin must not have been such a big deal to the kid, seeing as he backed out of his first big concert.' I don't think you should let him win."

I really meant it. I didn't care about the people out there, or the auditorium people who organized the evening. Right at that moment, I didn't even care about Arlene. I just wanted a guy who was my friend to go out on stage and stick it to his old man.

Jeremy didn't say anything for a while. I thought maybe he'd decided he just couldn't do it. And I wouldn't have blamed him.

"You want me to go tell them to make some kind of announcement? Maybe say you're sick or something?" I started for the door.

Jeremy looked up at me. "Would you do me a favor?"

I stopped and looked back at him. "Sure."

"I was wondering if maybe you could stay backstage with me."

I didn't get it. "What do you mean?"

"I'll play," Jeremy said. "But I'd appreciate it if you were in the wings. I mean, you don't have to." He shrugged like he was embarrassed to ask.

I grinned at him. "Are you kidding? Turn down the best seat in the house? No way I'd miss that."

"Okay. Then let's go."

Jeremy picked up his violin, and we walked out the door, down the hall and up a set of stairs that took us right beside the stage. As he was being introduced, he snuck one more peak out at the seats in the auditorium. Then he turned to me and shook his head. His dad wasn't there.

As Jeremy walked on stage, the audience cheered and whistled. I thought that was pretty cool at a classical music event. Jeremy stopped in front of the orchestra that was already on stage. And as the place became deathly silent, he began to play.

I didn't know the names of the pieces he played, but he finished with the Mendelssohn "Concerto in E Minor." I guess the conductor and

I were the only people in the place who knew Jeremy played the whole thing with tears rolling down his cheeks.

People talk about courage in sports. And they're right . . . it takes courage to go into the corner knowing you're going to get hit by a defenceman twice your size . . . and it takes courage to face a hundred-mile an hour fast ball, or drive a racecar, or ride a bucking bull. But what Jeremy Van Pelt—a skinny kid with a violin tucked under his chin—did that night took as much courage as any of that stuff.

Mr. Van Pelt got to the auditorium just in time for the reception they were having for Jeremy and the other musicians. He had a big stupid grin on his face. I don't think the guy had a clue that what he'd done that night was about as wrong as you can get. He went around the room and made sure everyone knew the game went into overtime, and that Chris had scored the winning goal.

The highlight of the evening was when he came over to where Arlene and I were standing. I was working on a cracker with some cream cheese and something I didn't recognize on it.

"Hey, Brad, I didn't know you were into this airy-fairy music."

My mouth was full so I couldn't answer, although I'm not sure what I would have said.

"Well, how about that kid of mine, eh?" he said to Arlene, with a big grin on his face.

"Which one, Mr. Van Pelt?" Arlene asked. "Or were you even aware that you had two?"

She turned and walked away.

Mr. Van Pelt looked at me. "That girl's parents need to teach her some manners."

"Have a cracker, Nick," I said, and I started off after Arlene. I turned back after a couple of steps. "Oh, and Nick ... I don't think you should be giving anybody advice on parenting."

When I got to Arlene she turned and high-fived me. But it got better. When we were sitting in the back seat of her parent's car on the way home, she reached over and took my hand. Then she turned toward me and said, "What you did tonight was very cool, Brad. You're a pretty special guy."

And she kissed me on the cheek. Right there in her parent's car! How cool is that?

15

Every year we finish off the season with a tournament. It isn't a big deal—not like going to Regionals or anything like that. Still, it's nice to win. Not that I would know how it feels to win that tournament, because the last time Lawrence had qualified for Regionals was twelve years ago—I wasn't even in kindergarten yet.

There were four teams in the tournament— the other three were Western Composite, St. Joseph's, and, of course, Central. We played St. Joseph's in our first game. We beat them 7-4. I got a couple of hits, but I also hit into two double plays. One of those "good news/bad news" games. My ankle didn't feel that bad. It had been pretty sore for about ten days, and I'd missed three games. I probably wouldn't have been much good in an Olympic hundred-meter sprint, but the good thing about being sort of slow is that nobody notices when you're even slower.

Central slaughtered Western 12-3, which meant we'd be playing Central in the Final. I had sort of hoped we'd meet up with Western again, just to see what Riverton's brother would do. But I didn't really think there was any way Western would beat Central. The worst thing was that Kincaid hadn't pitched. That meant he'd be rested, and ready for us. And after we beat them the last time we played them, I figured Central would be looking for revenge, big time.

Before the game, Coach Bunning came to me and asked me if I wanted to play. "That leg isn't one hundred per cent, and I'll understand if you want to sit this one out. I can always use you as a pinch hitter later in the game."

"Are you asking me, or telling me, Coach?"

"I'm asking you." He smiled as he said it.

"Good," I smiled back at him, "because you'd have to run me over with a bus to keep me out of this game."

During batting practice, I kept looking over at the area where Arlene had sat for our other games. She wasn't there yet, and I was starting to think that maybe she'd made up with Gary. I guess you can't really make up with somebody if you haven't actually broken up. As far as I knew, they were still going out, although Jeremy had told me things weren't perfect between them.

I think Jeremy was hoping for Arlene and me to get together. He wasn't the only one. But I wasn't sure I was getting anywhere. Oh, the kiss on the cheek in her parent's car was great. And I think she meant it about what I'd done to help Jeremy through his concert, which wasn't all that much, if you ask me. But when I called her, she had used that "let's just be friends" voice.

I took my turn at batting practice, and as soon as I was finished, I looked up into the stands again. Still no Arlene.

Coach Bunning called us over for a pre-game chat. "We know we're not going to get a lot of hits against this guy, so we're going to really work at generating a little offense," he told us. "When somebody gets on, we're going to bunt, steal, and hit-and-run. Let's have some fun with these guys."

We all whooped and hollered like you're supposed to after the coach gives you the "rah-rah" speech. Except this time I think every one of us felt like it. I have to admit, I liked his idea about trying to make things happen on the base paths. I figured it might be the only way to get by Central.

We were in the field first, so I went into the dugout to get my glove. When I came out, I started to run to first base. That's when I heard somebody call, "Brad."

This somebody wasn't just anybody—she was *the* somebody—Arlene Mitchell. I turned, and she was leaning over the railing behind first base. I ran over to her.

"Brad, I ... uh ... I'm sorry I haven't really been very nice when you've called me," she said.

"That's okay." I could see she was blushing, and heck, she'd said "uh" which I figured was a very good sign.

"I ... just wanted you to know I broke up with Gary. It was his idea for his brother to spike you.

He told me about it ... bragged about it. And ... uh ... well, I'd ... uh ... really like it if you wanted to phone me again sometime."

16

If we'd been anywhere but at a ballpark with several hundred fans in the bleachers, I'd have jumped up into the stands and hugged her till she couldn't breathe. But, of course, I couldn't do that. "I've got a better idea," I said. "How about some fries and a soda at Shakey's after the game?"

"Great," she said, and gave me that smile that I'd face Randy Johnson's fastball to see.

I ran out to first base, figuring I owned the world. One thing I was sure I owned was Dwight Kincaid. I couldn't wait to face him. I wasn't even worried when the Central Bears got a run in the first. I was sure I'd get that back single-handedly in the bottom of the first.

I was wrong about that. Kincaid struck out the side on eleven pitches. I was batting third, and I didn't even come close to catching up to his fastball. And things didn't get any better. Not in the second inning, or the third, or innings four through eight. Going into the ninth, we had two hits off the guy and I didn't have either one. I did manage to draw a walk in the fifth inning. I ended up wishing I hadn't.

I couldn't believe it when Coach Bunning gave me the steal sign. I stared at him like he was something off some sci-fi show. The thing is, I can't run. At least not very fast. French says I have deceptive speed—I'm even slower than I look. And he's probably right.

The last time I stole a base was in Little League. And they'd have nailed me that time, except the second baseman dropped the ball. But hey, when the skipper gives a sign, it's not my job to argue. He even went through the signs a second time, to make sure I got it.

On the first pitch, I took off for second like somebody had set fire to my underwear. I figured I was really moving. Maybe I was, but it wasn't even close. I was out by a bunch. And that was as close as we'd come to getting a runner into scoring position.

The only good thing about the game was that our pitchers had been awesome. John Neis had held the Bears to that one run they'd scored in the first inning. Ricky Lyons had come on in the seventh, and had mowed them down in order through the last three innings.

It was the bottom of the ninth, and it didn't look to me like Kincaid was weakening any. He got two quick strikes on our first hitter, Jeff Sandvick. But with a three and two count, Sandwich (Jeff had been called "Sandwich" for as long as I'd known him) got our third hit of the day. It was a little looper to right that dropped in.

French was up next, and I saw Coach Bunning give him the bunt sign. It was a good idea, since French is probably the fastest guy on the team. I moved into the on-deck circle to warm up. I'd be hitting after French.

French laid down a nice bunt, but Kincaid made a real nice play to get him at first base. Still, we had a runner at second for the first time in the game.

I stepped in with about as much confidence as a guppy in a tank full of piranhas. Kincaid blew the first one by me. It looked to me about as fast as the ones he'd been throwing back in the first inning. He missed with a curve, and then I fouled off a fastball. He missed with a fastball, and then I fouled off another one. I'd had a pretty good cut at that pitch, and my confidence got a little boost.

I stepped out and tapped my spikes. In that last game, he'd thrown me the fastball and I'd hurt him with it. He'd only thrown me one curve ball so far this at bat. If I was him, I'd be throwing another curve. Unless the ol' Kincaid ego got in the way, and he just had to get me with the heater. I figured after the last time, he'd put his ego aside.

I stepped in looking for the curve. This is it, man, I told myself. Here I was in another one of those Charlie Brown cartoons, where Charlie is either going to be the hero or the goat. With Charlie, it's always the goat.

Kincaid wound and delivered. I swung and made contact. I knew I'd hit it pretty good as soon as I felt it. Not good enough to get it out of the park, but decent. I watched it sail into right center. It looked like one of the fielders just might get to it.

But neither did. It bounced between them, and rolled to the fence. Sandwich scored easily. I took a peek at the outfield as I rounded second, and thought what the heck, why not go for third? Coach Bunning was signalling for me to stop at second, but I pretended I didn't see him. I even dived head first for the bag, something I've never done in my life.

And I was safe. A triple. As I got up and dusted myself off, I grinned at Coach Bunning who had that deer-in-the-headlights look on his face. "That was the game plan, wasn't it, Coach? Make something happen on the base paths?"

Coach Bunning shook his head. I doubt if he thought I was as funny as I thought I was. Our next hitter was Ricky Lyons. Ricky was not only our best pitcher, he could also hit. I figured we had a chance. If Ricky could get a hit or even a sacrifice fly, I'd get home with the winning run, and the celebration could begin. Of course, it would have to be a very deep sacrifice fly, because with my speed, something shallow or even medium-deep might not get it done. There I went, thinking like Charlie Brown again.

Kincaid went to two and one on Ricky. And that's when I got the shock of my life. Coach Bunning gave the squeeze bunt signal. I don't think Ricky could believe it either. He stepped out and looked at the Coach as he went through the signs again.

The thing about the squeeze is that the runner on third runs for home as soon as the bunt is down. It's a great play—especially if the guy on third is fast. It's not such a great play if the runner is slow to start with, and has an injured leg as well. If the bunt goes right to the pitcher, who then flips it to the catcher, a guy like me is pretty much history—and looks real stupid at the same time.

I looked at Coach Bunning again, but he wasn't looking at me. And he wasn't giving any more signals. The squeeze was on.

I suddenly felt like I was sweating more than I had the whole rest of the game. Maybe more than the whole rest of my life. Kincaid was in his wind-up. I took my leadoff, and watched Ricky. I tried not to think about all the bad things that could happen.

Kincaid let it go, and Ricky squared around to bunt. Things started to happen awful fast after that. Ricky bunted the ball and I ran. I ran down that baseline harder than I've ever run in my life.

But instead of everything happening fast, this time it was like everything went into slow motion, like in all those sports movies. I could see the ball was heading a little to the left of the mound. It wasn't a bad bunt, but it was a long way from perfect. Especially for a squeeze bunt, with a slow runner on third.

I could see out of the corner of my eye that Kincaid had got to the ball, and picked it up. I knew he'd be throwing to the catcher, good ol' Tom Cruz, who was parked in front of home plate, looking like a cement truck. I could sense that it was going to be close.

I slid. The first thing that got my attention was pain. It was like my lower leg—the same one Riverton had spiked—had just exploded.

The next thing I was aware of was the umpire sweeping his arm out to the sides and yelling,

"Safe!" I remember thinking that was a good thing. And I sort of remember hearing the crowd yelling, but I wasn't sure. It was about that time that I passed out.

17

When I woke up, I was on a stretcher. I lifted my head, and realized that some guys in smocks were carrying me toward an ambulance. The lights on the top of the ambulance were flashing.

That didn't make any sense. My leg was sore, and when I looked down at it, I could see a lot of blood around my ankle. So I'd torn open my stitches, so what?

I mean, don't get me wrong, there was a fair amount of pain (what people in the medical profession like to call "discomfort"). But other than that—and a pretty good headache from direct contact with Cruz's knee—I wasn't all that injured.

"Try not to move around too much," a voice said to me. Suddenly, it dawned on me this wasn't just any voice—this was the voice of the woman I love. I looked to my left, and sure enough, Arlene was walking beside the stretcher and holding my hand.

For a few seconds I thought about groaning a lot, and going for the sympathy thing, but I couldn't do it. "There's nothing wrong with me …let me off of this thing," I said.

"Just precautionary," one of the smock guys said. "You're probably just fine, but you're going to need sutures, and you took a pretty good knock on the head. We'll run you up to the hospital, and you'll probably be out in time for the victory celebration."

"Victory?" I repeated. "We won?"

"You were safe, Dude. It was a lousy slide, but you made it." Jeremy's grinning face appeared on my right.

"Thanks a lot." I said. "You criticize my sliding technique again and I'll tell you what I really think of your music."

His grin got bigger. "Hey, it looks to me like

things are working out just fine—considering you run bad and slide worse." He made a point of looking at my hand—the one Arlene was holding.

"Yeah, I guess you're right." I grinned back at him. Arlene gave my hand a little squeeze, which felt very nice.

"By the way, how are you doing, Buddy?" I hadn't seen Jeremy since his big concert.

The grin eased up a little, but didn't disappear altogether. "Feelin' great, actually. I figured out something. I figured out that I'm going to concentrate more on the people who like my music, and less on the people who don't. It's a piece of advice a friend gave me." The grin was back up to full speed again.

"Glad to hear it," I said.

"In fact, I'm feeling so good, I'm thinking of writing my first song. Yeah, I can see it now," Jeremy said, "I think I'll call it 'Teenage Love—Ain't it Sickening?'"

"Has a nice ring to it," I said. "I think it could be a huge hit."

"So do I." Arlene smiled at me as they slid me

into the ambulance. I noticed she was kind of slow to let go of my hand.

"I'll see you later at Shakey's," I told her.

"I hope so."

"You can bet on it." I smiled at her as they closed the ambulance door.

And you know something . . . I was there in one hour and eleven minutes. Who says I'm slow?